A Very Special Friend

By Dolores Cannon

Big Sandy Press®
P.O. Box 754, Huntsville, AR 72740 USA
www.ozarkmt.com

© 1981 by Dolores Cannon
1st Printing 2021, 2nd Printing 2022

All rights reserved. No part of this book, in part or in whole, may be reproduced, transmitted or utilized in any form or by any means, electronic, photographic or mechanical, including photocopying, recording, or by any information storage and retrieval system without permission in writing from Ozark Mountain Publishing, Inc. except for brief quotations embodied in literary articles and reviews.

For permission, serialization, condensation, adaptions, or for our catalog of other publications, write to Ozark Mountain Publishing, Inc., P.O. box 754, Huntsville, AR 72740, ATTN: Permissions Department.

Library of Congress Cataloging in Publication Data

Cannon, Dolores, 1931 - 2014

   A Very Special Friend, by Dolores Cannon

   This is a story of a young girl who was moved from where she grew up, to a new place in the country where she knew no one. Here she encounters a very special friend to help her adapt.

1. Imaginary Friend 2. Source 3. 4. Metaphysical 5. Coping

I. Cannon, Dolores, 1931 - 2014 II. Imaginary Friend III. Metaphysical IV. Title

Library of Congress Catalog Card Number: 2021942475

ISBN: 9781950639014

Cover Design: Victoria Cooper Art
Book set in: Times New Roman
Book Design: Summer Garr

Published under the imprint:

PO Box 754
Huntsville, AR 72740
WWW.OZARKMT.COM

Printd in the United States of America

Contents

Chapter One
The Meeting 1

Chapter Two
What Is Magic? 17

Chapter Three
The Hornet's Nest 27

Chapter Four
The Snake 35

Chapter Five
Sandy Gets Into Mischief 45

Chapter Six
The Ducks and the Turtle 55

Chapter Seven
The Icy Winter 67

Chapter Eight
The Parting 81

About the Author 89

Illustrations
Sandy (on Title Page) by Dolores Cannon
All other illustrations by Daria Kilochko

Chapter One
THE MEETING

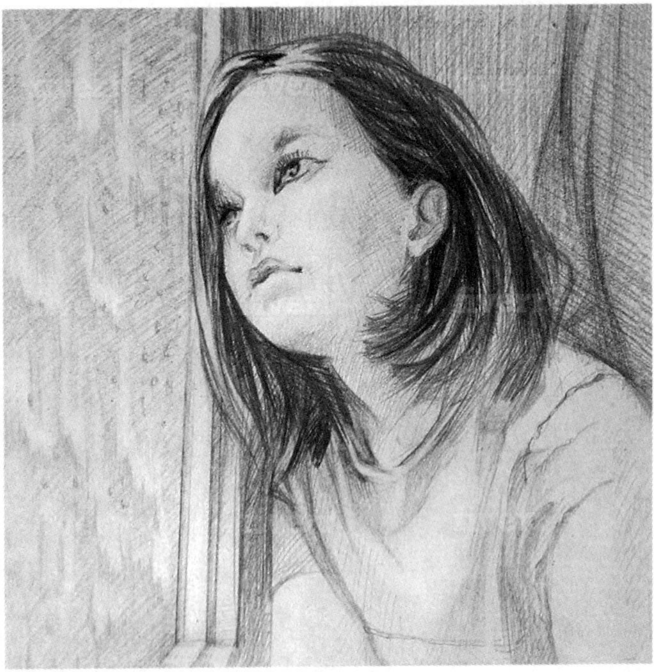

The Meeting

Nancy sat solemnly at the window, watching the raindrops roll steadily down the panes. The weather was just right, because to her the raindrops were all the teardrops she had been unable to let out since moving here to the country. She had been so sad since moving here, but she couldn't let her mother and father know. They would feel too bad. They thought they were doing the best thing for all the family when they decided to move away from the big city. They thought there wouldn't be so many problems living near a small town, and they would be able to grow most of their food. Nancy thought they were probably right, but on a day like this all she could think about was her best friend, Jeanne.

Why didn't parents understand about how it was between her and Jeanne. They had promised to be friends forever, but how was that possible now with about a thousand miles between them. They had told each other all the deep important secrets that you keep hidden way down in your heart. The ones that no one else can ever know and parents can never understand. But now, here she was in a strange house in a strange part of the country, with no one. She had never felt so lonely in all of her ten years of growing up.

The place they had picked was on top a big sandy mountain. The people called it that because the soil was like the sand of a seashore. In fact, millions of years ago it <u>was</u> a seashore. There were limestone deposits in the valley below where a huge ocean used to be, but that was long before any people lived here in Arkansas. In fact, no one had lived on the land they had bought for fifty years. So her parents were kept busy with all the work it takes to try to turn a house into a home. Of course, she was busy too, helping with the work, but that didn't matter on a day like today, when all she could think about was the way things used to be.

It wasn't bothering her brother, Tommy, but then he was bigger, almost teenage. He was allowed to drive the old car around the dirt roads, something he would never have been allowed to do yet in the city; so he felt quite important. He had already begun to make friends and find things to do, but who wants a little kid sister tagging along. Her mother kept telling her not to worry, that school would be starting in a few months and she would make lots of friends then. But here it was, only the middle of summer and school seemed a long time away. Why didn't parents understand how frightening it was to start a new school where you didn't know anyone at all. At the old school she knew everybody. Maybe here she would never fit in. Maybe she would always be the new girl. Maybe no one would ever like her. If only she could have just <u>one</u> friend to talk to, things wouldn't seem so bad.

With a deep sigh, Nancy pressed her head against the glass, and from the corner of her eye she saw a quick movement of something outside. A fleeting glimpse of something ..... red. Red? "Must have been a cardinal," she thought, and went back to her daydreaming.

The rain had ended by bedtime, and a brilliant full moon slid out from behind the clouds. The

The Meeting

golden light filled Nancy's room and made it almost as light as day. As the light fell across her bed, she awakened with a start. She lay there trying to figure out what had awakened her. Was it the light? No, there was something else ... different ... out-of-place. She looked around the room. The soft light lit up all her familiar toys and objects as they sat in their usual places. The only difference she could see was the dream-like appearance they had taken on. No, nothing in the room had changed. What was it then?

Wait! There it was again! It was a sound, a sound that had awakened her. That was what was out-of-place. But what was it? Where was it coming from? It wasn't the drone of the crickets and the hum of the night-bugs that usually lull you to sleep in the country. That sound had softened and could barely be heard. No, it sounded more like singing! Nancy was used to the beautiful call of the whippoorwill at night. Sometimes they came near the house and could get quite loud at times. No, this was different. It was singing, but not like anything she had ever heard before. It had a beautiful clear sound of a tinkling bell, yet very faint.

She got out of bed and went to the window to look for the source. The remains of the rain sparkled in small puddles on the lawn as the moon slipped in and out of the clouds, casting strange shadows everywhere. A dozen golden fireflies blinked and danced against the dark background, looking like little stars fallen from the sky. Suddenly, she caught a movement. There was something out there! As the moon went in and out, she could make out the shape of something running and jumping over the puddles. All the while, the faint sound of singing; clear, sparkling, more like a tiny bell than anything she had ever hear. But what was it out there?

Nancy rubbed her eyes as the moon suddenly lit up a small figure dancing on the lawn. "Why!" she gasped, "it looks like a little person!" It definitely wasn't a bird or animal. She could make out a head and arms and legs. She soon realized it was nothing to fear as she caught a glimpse of the whimsical expression on its face. She lay her head down on the windowsill to watch its antics as it ran and jumped and danced. How strange! What was it and where did it come from? She thought, "I'll wonder about it tomorrow," and closed her eyes to listen to the beautiful little song as it went on and on.

The Meeting

The sun streaming in the window woke her the next morning. She was still by the window. "What am I doing here? Did I sleep here last night? Maybe I walked in my sleep?"

Then as she looked out the window at the birds playing in the rain puddles, she remembered. "That was sure a strange dream I had last night."

One thing about living in the country, if you want peace and quiet, it isn't very hard to find. Everyone needs a place of their very own where they can be alone to think thoughts and dream dreams. Nancy's brother, Tommy, had already found "his" place. It was a small cave and he was planning cookouts and campouts there this fall with his new friends. Well, Nancy had found "her" place also. A little spring back in the woods surrounded by ferns and moss-covered rocks. She liked to go back there when she wanted to be alone, sit with her back against a tree and read. So, on this day she was walking through the woods, book in hand, to "her" place. At least she could think her own private thoughts, even if she had no one to share them with.

Squirrels and rabbits ran away from her, and birds twittered noisily overhead as she walked through the trees. Then she heard another sound, it seemed to be coming from the direction of her spring. It was such a soft sound that someone else might have missed it all together, but it sounded like someone crying. She crept slowly up to a large tree and peeked around. She couldn't believe her eyes as she saw where the sound was coming from.

Seated on a rock, almost hidden by the ferns around him, was a little creature. He appeared human-like, but he was so small. The most noticeable feature was a mass of red hair that was so unruly it stuck out in all directions. The little thing sat with his tiny hands covering his face, and he was crying as though his little heart would break.

Nancy felt no fear of the creature, because there was absolutely nothing to be afraid of. He looked so unhappy. He obviously didn't know she was there. She dropped her book and blurted out, "It wasn't a dream. You're the one I saw dancing on the lawn! You're real, after all!"

At the sound of her voice the little being jumped up with a sharp gasp and tried to hide behind the ferns. "Don't go away!" she said pleadingly. "Please don't go away. I want to talk to you."

The mop of red hair peeked out from among the leaves, and a little piping, high-pitched voice said, "You mean you can see me? You can _really_ see me?"

"Of course I can. I'm talking to you, aren't I?"

He crept slowly and cautiously out and sat on the rock again. "Yes, you are. But I've always believed that people couldn't see me. At least, they have always acted like they couldn't. Of course, living here in the woods like I do, I haven't seen very many humans. Most of my friends are the birds and animals and we're all pretty used to each other. Sometimes we see people, but they are usually the ones who come to hurt the animals, and they carry those long stick-like things that make lots of noise."

He didn't seem to be afraid of her anymore as he cocked his head from side to side to study her.

"Oh, you must mean a gun. Those were probably hunters." Nancy said.

"Well, whatever they are, the creatures of the woods are always very afraid when they come, so I thought that all people would hurt us. But for some reason they never seemed to be able to see me. That makes it easier for me to warn my friends when I see people coming. You aren't like that, are you? Do you have one of those guns, those noisy things?"

Nancy laughed, "No, I don't have one. Don't worry, I wouldn't hunt you. She was absolutely delighted to be talking to this tiny thing, but she was also curious. "Tell me, why were you crying when I came up just now?"

He hung his head and blushed, "Well, I'm embarrassed to tell you. – I always thought I was happy living here with my friends. I have been here as long as I can remember and never knew there was anything different. But then, you and your family moved in and I have been watching you. I suddenly realized something is missing, and I got so lonely I couldn't help crying."

Nancy couldn't believe her ears. "You, you are lonely? How can that be? It is so beautiful and peaceful here in the woods, and you have so many friends. I have been so lonely because I had to leave my friends and I have no one to talk to."

He laughed, "Well, I can't believe that! I think you are making fun of me. How can people be lonely? There are so many of you, you have each other. I've watched you. You have your family to talk to all the time. Me? I suddenly realized that I am one of a kind. I've never seen anybody else

The Meeting

like me. Yes, I can talk with the animals. They can't talk like you, but I can understand them. But really, they're a little dumb. They are selfish too, thinking only about finding something to eat and about their own little groups. I've had a terrible time trying to teach them to live together. Sometimes they listen and sometimes they don't. I suppose I shouldn't talk like that about them, because they are my friends, after all. But when I saw you, I thought how nice it would be to share my thoughts with someone who could talk back. You're a lot more like me than they are, except that you are so big."

"Isn't that funny," Nancy said, "That's the same thing I was thinking about. Gosh, it would be wonderful if we could be friends and talk together. Then neither one of us would be lonely anymore. – But I don't even know your name."

"Name? What's a name?"

"That's what we call each other," Nancy looked puzzled. "It's who or what you are."

"Does everything have to be called something, to be a who or a what? I'm just me. I've always been me. Nobody ever called me anything."

Nancy thought, "Well, I guess we people have to have names for each other or it would be awfully hard to tell us apart. – My name is Nancy."

He frowned, "I guess people aren't as smart as I thought they were. You must need names because you haven't learned how to look inside and see the real person yet. That's the real you, not a name. But I guess if you have to call me something, just pick out something."

Nancy was deep in thought, "How about Ralph? – Sidney? – No? – Well, you say you have been here as long as you can remember, so you are really a part of the life on Big Sandy Mountain. What do you think of the name like Sandy?"

He shook his little red head. "Well, I guess if you have to give everything a name, that one's as good as any other." He let out a big sigh. "I guess I can live with it."

"Sandy," Nancy smiled. "I like the sound of it anyway." Then her brow furrowed. "But Sandy, what are you doing here all by yourself? Why aren't there more of you?"

"Well, I've wondered about that many times myself. And when I do, the All-Over Spirit talks to me and tries to make me understand."

Nancy interrupted, "The Who?"

Sandy looked a little puzzled for a moment. "Don't tell me you don't know <u>Him</u>? I thought you would know more than I ever could. He's the one that kind of runs everything. The guy in charge. I can understand why people can't see me, because I can't see <u>Him</u>. I call Him the All-Over Spirit because He seems to be everywhere. He is really more of a voice, although you feel it more than you hear it. But it's always very clear. You know just what you're supposed to do. Well, He told me one day that I'm here alone because I'm supposed to help with nature, the animals and the birds. There aren't very many of us. We are kind of special and He didn't make very many. I'm not supposed to interfere, just try to help, especially to get them to live peacefully together. But sometimes I don't think I'm doing a very good job, because they don't always listen to me. They just go on and do what they want to do. He gave me a lot of jobs to do, and I'm trying, but I'm not very good at anything yet."

Nancy laughed, "That sounds a lot like me. Everyone in our family can do something, but I can't seem to do anything right. My Mom tells me not to worry, that someday I'll find my own special thing. She says everyone can do something. – What kind of jobs do you have to do?"

He frowned, "Well, like I said, the ones He gave me aren't easy. I'm still learning and sometimes I mess up the job. My main one is: Every morning I have to get my bucket of water and go around and put the dewdrops on the leaves and spider webs. Of course, the water evaporates every day so I have to do it again the next morning."

"Why do you have to do that?"

Sandy shook his head. "You sound just like those spiders. That's the same thing they ask me. It gets them angry because it makes their web slippery. So I'll tell you the same thing I was told: Does everything have to have a reason? Can't some things just exist for the sake of beauty? The pleasure it gives you to look at it?"

"I never thought of it like that before."

Sandy folded his arms in a huff. "Well, I sure hope all my work won't be for nothing. I hope someone sees the beauty in it. – I tried painting the leaves in the fall, but I kept spilling the paint. You know, it's not easy climbing around on the trees and trying to carry paint cans too. So, He said He would take care of it until I got the hang of my other jobs. He said, don't worry, He will never give me more than I can handle."

Nancy cupper her face in her hands. "Gee, Sandy, you are so wise. I don't think I could be so smart if I lived to be a hundred. You must be very old. How old are you anyway?"

"There you go again, naming things. Old? What is old? What is time anyway? I think that's something you humans make up to make things more complicated than they already are. Old? I don't know. I said I've been here as long as I can remember. Time? One day follows the other. The sun goes around. It is light, and it is dark. It is warm in the summer and it is cold in the winter. Why do we have to draw lines and make limits? Why can't you just enjoy everything He has put here and don't worry about time, about tomorrow? Why don't you people just slow down and look around you? There is so much beauty and it's all there for you to see. That's one thing I have observed about you people, you always seem to be in a hurry."

Suddenly the quiet of the woods was shattered by a voice calling from the house. Nancy jumped; it was unexpected. She had become so engrossed in what Sandy was saying. "Oh, I will have to go. That's my Mom calling me for supper. Will I see you again? Please, Sandy, say I can see you again."

Sandy thought for a moment. "I guess so. I get the feeling that you will be able to see me as long as you need me. I don't know what will happen after that. I feel that I probably will not have anything to say about it. But I'm always around. If you want me, just call me."

Jumping up and waving good-bye, Nancy reluctantly ran towards the house. Glancing back over her shoulder, she could still make out a splash of red against the rock.

Chapter 2
What Is Magic?

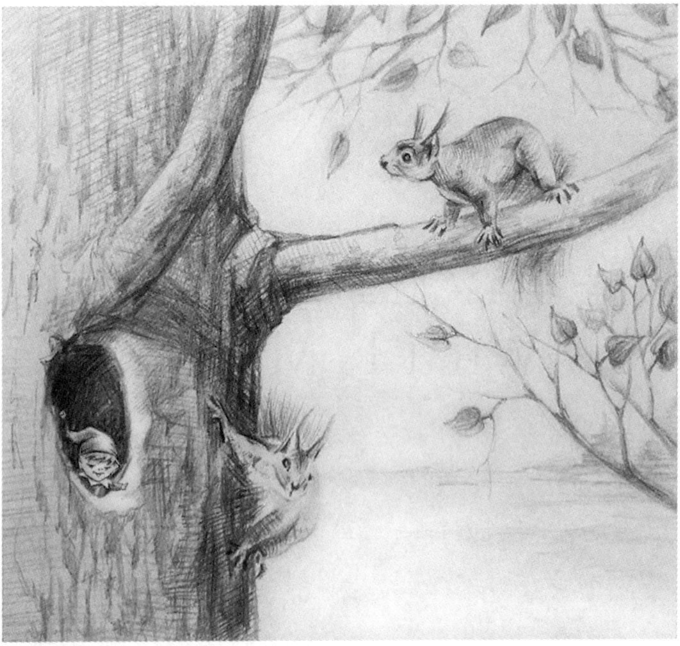

What Is Magic?

The next day as soon as Nancy had finished her chores, she took off in a run back through the woods. She went to the spring and looked for Sandy. She couldn't see him anywhere. She called and called, a little afraid that maybe he wouldn't come. Maybe she would never see him again. Then she heard a little high-pitched voice answer. But it seemed to be coming from overhead. Shading her eyes, she looked up at the trees and branches. Then she saw him, a little mop of red hair sticking out of a hole in the hollow tree nearby.

She ran over to the tree. "Oh, Sandy, I was afraid I wouldn't find you again."

He yawned, "Oh, I'm here. I don't go very far away. But I didn't get much sleep last night, so I didn't hear you at first."

"What on earth are you doing there in that hollow tree?" She had to stand on tiptoe to see him.

"Oh, this is where I live. I tried an old bird nest once, it was fine until it rained. Then I found this." He ducked back inside and told her to look in the hole. She could see a mat made of leaves, pine needles and many other things Sandy had probably picked up around the woods.

Nancy said, "It looks vey nice. You're probably quite comfortable in there."

"I guess so. It's all right most of the time. But you see, I've got a pair of squirrels for neighbors upstairs." He pointed. "Up there in the other hole. And sometimes – last night, for instance – they can really get noisy. Chatter, chatter, chatter.

And they get to running around in there. Then all kinds of stuff started falling down on my head, mostly their old empty nut shells. I didn't think they'd ever go to sleep. You know I have to get up early with my job. Some people don't think about anything but themselves. Well, after I got back from putting out the dewdrops, I thought I'd go back to bed for a little while, but no such luck." He was half sprawled out of the hole; he eyes half open.

"Why, what happened then? Did the squirrels start in again?" She was suddenly interrupted by a loud rat-a-tat-tat-bang-bang. The whole hollow tree shook. "What on earth is that?" she asked, her eyes wide with surprise.

He didn't even have to look, he just pointed upward. "It's just him. He's back again. Can't you see him up there? It's the woodpecker. He's my friend, but today I feel more like he's a pest."

She shaded her eyes and looked up. There near the top of the tree sat a beautiful large woodpecker, pecking away at the old bark. He had black and white feathers and a red pointed head. He would bang away look down at Sandy and then start banging again.

"He's beautiful. I don't think I have ever seen a woodpecker as large as that. But what does he want?"

"Well, it isn't his fault really. We have gotten into a habit. Almost every morning when the weather is good, he comes and takes me for a ride. He helped me find this place to live. He pecked the hole out big enough for me to climb in and out. And he made little hollows on the side of the tree for steps, so I could get up and down easily. One day I had to go someplace that was farther away, and he knew I couldn't walk that far, so he offered me a ride. It was so much fun, and I enjoyed it so much, that we have been doing it ever since. But he doesn't seem to understand. I didn't get much sleep last night and I don't really want to go today. Besides, now that you're here I'd rather talk with you." He cocked his head and looked up at his friend, the bird. Nancy could hear soft twittering and then the woodpecker flew away. "Okay, he said he would come back tomorrow. He's afraid of you. He doesn't like to get too close to a human."

"Well, I won't hurt him. He's too pretty."

Sandy climbed out and sat on the edge of the hole. "I know that, but he isn't too sure yet. Animals and birds have learned it is just better not to trust humans."

Nancy's brow furrowed. "You know, Sandy, I've been doing a lot of thinking about you. I haven't got you figured out yet. Now I'm more confused than ever. If you ride around on the back of a bird, you must not be able to fly by yourself. I thought you had to be magic. Just what can you do anyway?"

He looked surprised. "What do you mean, what can I do? What can you do? People can do anything if they want to bad enough. Nothing is impossible for those who believe. It's all right there in your mind. Thoughts are very powerful. That's why you must be very careful not to think about bad things that will hurt others. But if you can picture it in your mind and believe enough, you can do anything. Maybe that's why you were able to see me, because you wanted somebody badly enough. These things are so easy for me to understand, I thought you people already knew about them too. But I see that you don't, so I guess I'll just have to teach you."

"But Sandy, that's not what I mean. Elves and fairies that I've read about in my books are little people like you, and they are all magic. They have secret powers."

He cocked his head, and said with a twinkle in his eye, "All the secret power you will ever need is hidden inside you. As for magic? It's all around you, and you probably have never even really noticed it."

Nancy looked puzzled. "All around! But Sandy, I don't understand."

He climbed down from the tree. "Oh, boy, you humans! I got more than I bargained for when I got mixed up with you! Okay, sit down here and I'll try to explain a few things to you." He sat on the moss next to her and continued. "Have you ever listened to the whisper of the wind as it blows though the branches? It sounds almost as though the trees are talking to each other. Or how about the patter of the raindrops as they fall on the leaves, and the sweet smell of the earth when it gets wet? And when the rain is over, have you ever seen a rainbow? And then the sun breaking through the clouds makes all kinds of patterns on the ground as it shines through the leaves of the trees. These are some of the most magical, beautiful things I know of."

"No, I guess most people are just too busy to notice things like that. When it rains, all I think about is that I can't go outside, or I'll get wet. I'm usually just glad when the rain is over. I guess most of us just think of rain as a nuisance."

"A nuisance?" He stomped his little foot. "Let me show you what happens after a rain. Lift up that pile of dead leaves over there. See the little green leaves and yellow flowers poking their way up from the dirt? And, that little acorn there. That's where that big oak tree over there started from. How could any of it happen without the rain? You talk about magic, that's real magic!"

He jumped up and ran over to another tree. "Come here. You want magic, I'll show you magic!" She followed meekly over to see what Sandy was pointing at.

There in the crook of a branch was a bird's nest. "What do you mean? All I see is a bird's nest."

"Well, then open your eyes. You people look at things, but you don't seem to see anything." He said in a huff. "Is there anything in the nest?"

"Why, yes, there are four little eggs!" Then Nancy's attention was drawn to a blue jay sitting nearby fussing and hollering at her.

"Well, I want you to carefully pick one of them up and hold it in your hand." Nancy hesitated as she glanced at the angry bird. "Don't worry about her. I'll explain to her that you're not going to hurt them. – Well, tell me what you think."

She stood quietly holding the little egg in her hand. Then suddenly her eyes flew open in surprise and she gasped. "Why, I feel something. There's something moving inside the shell."

"Yes, that's the baby bird. It will be hatching soon. There you have the greatest magic of all. The magic of life! Why don't people understand that it is the most wonderful thing in the world. Why must they wait until it is too late to really appreciate it?"

Sandy went over and climbed back up into his hollow tree. He sat at the entrance and yawed.

"I think I'll try to get another little nap before those squirrels get back from hunting nuts. You need time to think about what I told you anyway. You people seem to get confused if I try to tell you too much."

He disappeared back inside the hole as Nancy walked away, deep in thought. A butterfly danced in front of her, the sunlight shining from the many colors in its wings. "Magic!" she thought out loud.

Chapter 3
The Hornet's Nest

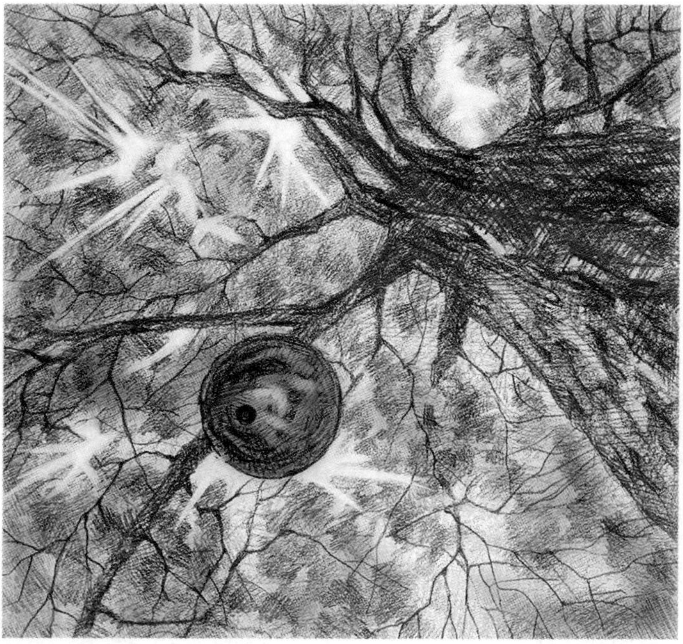

"Hey, wait for me, Nancy!" Sandy yelled as he ran and jumped and tried to catch up with her. "You take such big steps; I can't keep up with you."

Nancy turned around with a start. "Oh, Sandy, I didn't see you. You're usually back in the woods. I can't go back there today. The folks left, and I have things to do here before they get back. So, I'll probably be busy all day. – but maybe I can sit down out here for just a little bit."

They went over to a large tree that grew near the house. The tree had long spreading branches and made a very good shade tree; besides the grass looked very inviting. So, Nancy laid down under the tree as Sandy perched on a nearby rock. She confided in Sandy that since she had met him, she didn't seem to miss her friend Jeanne as much anymore. She didn't think it meant she didn't love her anymore. She thought that having Sandy to talk to just made it easier.

Looking up at the sunlight shining through the leaves, she suddenly let out a gasp and sat upright. "Look, up in the tree! There's something big and dark up there!"

Sandy looked upward. "Oh, haven't you seen that before? It's just a hornet's nest. Big one, isn't it?"

"A hornet's nest!" Nancy screamed and jumped up, ready to run.

"Don't you know? Everyone is afraid of hornets. I've seen movies and cartoons all my life about people being chased by them. They're bad and mean. Hornets sting, don't they?"

"I've figured out that you people are so afraid of everything because you don't understand things. Do you even try to understand? Think about it. That nest is so large it must have been there all summer. If they haven't bothered you yet, why should they bother you now?"

Nancy cautiously sat back down, still keeping a wary eye on the dark shape over her head. "You know, you're probably right. We all have walked under this tree a hundred times. Tommy was fooling around with that old car right under this tree. We didn't even know it was here."

"Maybe they have not bothered you because you have not bothered them. As long as you don't mean them any harm, why should they hurt you? They have their own life to live, their own part in the order of things. There is no reason why you can't live peacefully together. Most creatures won't hurt humans. If they are given a chance, they would prefer to stay as far away from humans as possible. They live better in their own world without the humans. Some of the creatures don't always behave the way I would like, but the All-Over Spirit made everything for a reason. Nothing is all bad. It has its reason for being here. Humans seem to be afraid of everything, and they always try to hurt what they don't understand. When humans start messing up the order of things, that's when we usually have trouble.

"You may be right, because I was just thinking how we could get rid of them. I couldn't do it, because I would be too scared, but I was wondering how my folks would go about it. I know when they see it, they might try poison or burning it."

Sandy shook his head sadly. "But don't you see? If they tried something like that, then the hornets would have to defend their home, and someone would probably get hurt. I don't think you should tell your folks yet. Maybe by the time they find it they will understand that it has been there a long time and it hasn't caused anybody any trouble. Why don't people try to learn from things in nature, instead of just destroying what they don't understand?"

"What do you mean? How can you learn from nature?" She looked puzzled.

"Well, you don't have to be foolish about it, just learn to respect it. Don't do anything to frighten them, like bumping their nest. They will only be around for a few more months, so learn to appreciate their beauty."

"Ugh," Nancy frowned. "How can such a thing be beautiful?"

Sandy put his hands on his hips and sighed. "Here we go again. Stand up, and I want you to look at it. Open your eyes and really see it." As Nancy hesitated, "Go ahead. They will not hurt you. They're too busy with their own business."

Nancy stood up and gazed at the nest about two or three feet above her head. "Why, it's made out of something that looks like paper. And there's one bee sitting at the entrance looking at me. He looks something like a wasp, but he has a white face. How do they make that paper-like stuff?"

"They get their building materials from old wood. Sometimes you can see them over there on your porch. It's made out of rough wood, and that's perfect for them. That's probably why they decided to build so close to your house. There's plenty of material for them to use. They strip tiny pieces of wood off and chew it up. They turn it into paper and glue it together somehow to make the nest. It's a hard job and takes a lot of them to just keep the nest repaired. The wind and rain are always tearing pieces off, so they keep busy just working on the nest. They have a queen and workers, just like all the other bees."

"Oh, yes, I know about queens and worker bees, because we have a hive of honeybees. My Dad wanted them. He said you need bees in order to have fruit trees and a good garden. – But you said that they would only be around for a few months. Our honeybees are there all the time, my Dad said."

"Yes, and the odd thing about that is the honeybees are the only ones who stay in the hive all winter. With the hornet, the queen is the only one who survives the winter. At the first signs of frost or winter coming, she leaves the hive and hibernates in a dead log or some other rotting wood."

"Well," Nancy said, "I don't think that's a very good queen. I thought a ruler was supposed to take care of her people. Won't they all die without her?"

"Yes, the rest of the hive will die. Apparently,

they don't know she's gone, or think she's coming back, because they keep right on working. Do you know that a bee really just works itself to death? But gradually, without her to lay more eggs to replace the dying workers, the colony just dwindles away. They keep working until the end, but finally the cold weather kills off the rest. It seems cruel, but there are a lot of things in nature that seem cruel. I don't understand the reasons for everything, but I know that there has to be a reason. The All-Over Spirit is probably the only one who really knows, because He made them."

"You know," said Nancy thoughtfully, "when you really look at it, it is beautiful. I would have been scared to death to get this close to one before, because I figured they would hurt me. That's what I've always been taught. But it really is amazing that those little insects can make something so complicated. Maybe you're right, there must be lots of other things that are around us every day just waiting for somebody to notice them and say, 'Gee, you're beautiful!'. But most of the time we're just too busy to look at them. I guess it's like you said, we look but we don't really see. – I think I would like to have that nest to hang in my room. Without the hornets, of course. I don't think they would understand living in a house. And I wouldn't want to take it until they were finished with it and didn't need it anymore."

"Well," said Sandy, "if you do decide to keep it, don't wait too long. Sooner or later the birds will tear it apart to eat the dead hornets. If you notice, you don't find these nests very often.

That's why. The birds get hungry in the winter and they know there is food in there."

"I think if I tell my folks all that you told me; they will be interested too. Maybe they will decide not to destroy it and let me keep it. I hope so. But how can we tell when it's safe to take it down?"

"If you watch, you'll see that the hornets won't be so active. That means that more and more of them are dying. It will probably be safe when the days get colder. I'll tell you when. But one way to get it would be to put a bag of some kind over it and cut the limb. If any are still alive, they will probably be too weak and cold to hurt you. Be sure you tie the top of the bag shut. A safe place to hang it would be in the shed over there. That would be cold this winter. If you bring it in the house too soon, some of them might wake up and they would probably be confused and angry. If it hangs in the shed until next spring it should be safe to take inside the house."

"That would be a good idea," she said. "It might be fun to watch it grow, now that I know it won't hurt me. I wonder how big it will get before the hornets get tired. – I would like to have it in the house. Then it would be there to remind me of what you said, about having to really look close at things sometimes to see the beauty there."

Chapter 4
THE SNAKE

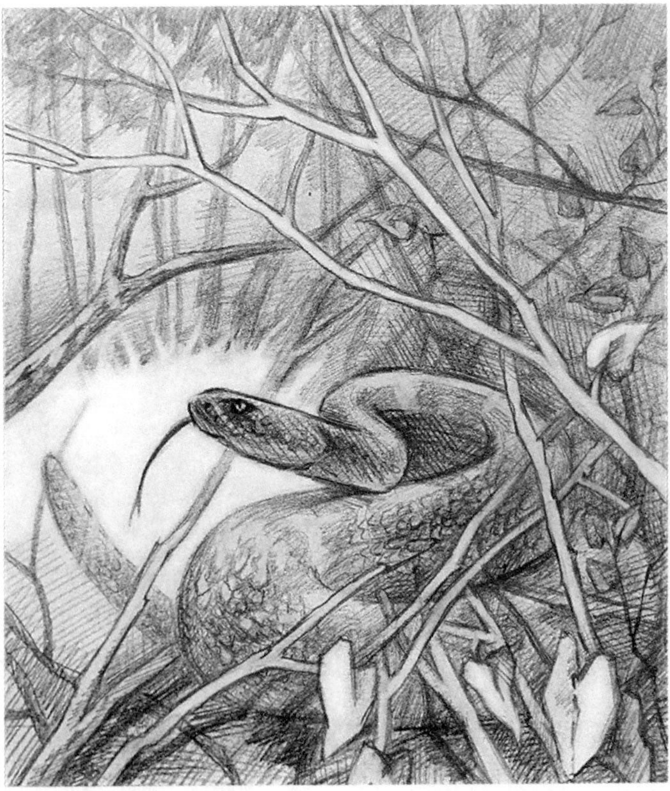

The Snake

Sandy and Nancy were busy looking for eggs. It was difficult to keep all the chickens inside the pen. There were always some who wanted to be different, or maybe they just liked to make things hard for people. Whatever the reason, they would get out, hide their nests and lay their eggs in the oddest places. Maybe they just wanted to raise a batch of babies, and the only way to do it was to hide the eggs so people wouldn't keep taking them. Nancy thought it was fun to look for them, like an Easter egg hunt. She had already found some, and she knew her mother would be pleased. Of course, Sandy was a big help. He was so small he could crawl under and behind things a lot easier than a human could.

They were moving branches around in an old brush pile when suddenly there was a rustling sound down underneath. As Nancy carefully moved the branches aside, she was surprised to see a snake coiled to strike. She screamed. Because Sandy was nearer, it made a loud hiss and struck at him. He let out a surprised yelp and jumped back a few feet. "Boy, he scared me! I didn't see him!"

Nancy had backed away too. "He scared you! I didn't think you were afraid of anything."

"I never did say that! I understand creatures here in the woods, and I have a lot of respect for them. But there are some that even I have to be careful with. Snakes are one of them. They are very hard to talk to, and you know they can't see very good. So, they just strike at anything, and worry about it later. I don't think they have very many friends with an attitude like that."

Nancy was looking around for a stick. "What should we do now? Should I go get my folks? They could kill it with a hoe or something."

"You don't have to kill it. I know this kind and they won't hurt you." As he said that the snake struck again, all the time waving his head back and forth and hissing loudly. His tongue darted in and out rapidly. Sandy put his hands on his hips, "Now, you just cut that out!"

Nancy's eyes were wide, "What do you mean, he won't hurt you? What do you think he's trying to do?"

"Oh, he's just bluffing. He's putting on a front, pretending to be something he isn't."

"But aren't all snakes bad? Whenever we first came here Mom made us wear those old heavy boots any time we went outside. She was sure there was a snake under every rock. We didn't see very many, but they killed everyone anyway just to be on the safe side. We haven't seen any lately, so we don't have to wear those boots anymore."

"Well," Sandy nodded, "some snakes can hurt you. I know that because I have to watch out for them too. Some are very touchy and not friendly at all. But they aren't *all* bad. Some of them actually help people by killing rats and mice. Mostly a snake just wants to be left alone. Now this fellow here, he is acting so strange because he isn't poisonous and doesn't have any other way of defending himself. So, he thinks he can put on a big bluff and scare people into leaving him alone. He has a pattern on his body and lots of people think that means he is poisonous but look at his eyes."

"*You* look at his eyes. I'm not going to get that close to him!"

"What I mean is," Sandy continued, "his eyes look like yours and mine, with a round pupil. A poisonous snake has eyes that look like your cat, with a slit pupil. But let me show you what else this fellow can do."

He danced around in front of the snake and began to make fun of it. The snake's body began to sway back and forth, the black tongue daring in and out, and he struck again. But the odd thing was that it didn't seem to open its mouth when it struck at the dancing little figure. "Oh, you're just an old bluffer, that's what you are," Sandy taunted. "You don't scare me. I'm on to you. – Now, Nancy, watch what he does with his head."

As she stared, the snake began to puff out the sides of its neck and head and flatten it out. "Why, he looks like the pictures I've seen of cobras. But cobras don't live here in Arkansas."

"You know what you look like? Look, I can do it too!" Sandy puffed and blew his little cheeks out until they were red. "that's what you look like, and it doesn't scare me." He stopped and caught his breath. "You see, his only defense is to imitate all the other snakes and make everyone afraid of him."

As Nancy watched, the snake suddenly fell to the ground, rolled over on its back and lay as though it were dead, with its tongue sticking out of its mouth. "What happened? Did he faint? But how can a snake faint? Do you think he was really so scared that he just fainted? Or is he dead?"

"No, he didn't faint. He's just faking. It's just one more thing he can pull out of his bag of tricks. He saves it till last if he can't scare you away. He makes you think he's dead. I guess he figures you won't bother him if he's dead."

She leaned over to look at the snake more closely. "Are you sure? He's not moving. He sure looks dead to me."

"Okay, I'll prove it to you. Take a stick and turn him back over on his stomach." He watched as Nancy carefully flipped the snake back over. Then it did a strange thing. It flopped over again onto its back with its tongue sticking out. Nancy's eyes were wide with amazement.

"Why, you're right. He is an old faker." She laughed.

"You can even pick him up with a stick and carry him around like that, and he'll still act like he's dead. Then when he's got you good and fooled and you walk away, do you know what he does?" Nancy shook her head. "Well, then he will escape so fast you can hardly believe it. Yes, I guess he acts strange, but it's the only way to save his life sometimes. Just scare people and confuse them and they'll leave him alone. He can't help it because that's the way he was made. But aren't there people like that too?"

"I see what you mean. Yes, I've seen people

that are that way. Sometimes the kids at school act like that too. I guess they're afraid that people won't like them the way they really are, so they pretend to be something they aren't. They make believe, make up things about themselves and even lie to impress people. But I've noticed that most of the time the teachers aren't fooled. A lot of times the other kids get to where they don't like them either. I guess they really don't fool anyone for very long. Why do you think they do that, Sandy?"

"I guess it's like you said, they're afraid that people won't like them the way they really are. They have to make themselves sound different and exciting. They haven't learned about the real 'you'. The real part of everyone that is so beautiful and wonderful. That part of a person is different from any other person. There are no two alike, I guess they haven't learned how to let that part of them shine through. If they did, they might find out people would like them the way they really are, without all the made-up stuff, the tricks. Just like that snake, in the end the only one they fool is themselves. People like that must be very lonely. I guess you have to feel sorry for them. When people start telling lies, it must get very complicated. How can they remember who they told what lie to? I think if you just stick to telling the truth, it's much easier. At least you don't have to remember everything you say."

Nancy seemed lost in thought. "I guess that's really why I haven't been able to tell anybody about you yet, Sandy. I'm afraid they won't believe me. They would probably think I was lying or trying to get attention. I know you haven't come around much when my folks are all here. But there are times, like when you peck on my window, that I think they would surely notice you. It's really very strange."

"No, Nancy." He frowned. "They probably can't see me because they don't need me. They are all so busy, and they have each other, so they don't need to see me. You're right though, I don't think you should tell them about me. They might make fun of you, and that would hurt me to see it. Sometimes I get a little worried and scared."

"You?" she gasped in disbelief. "What could you be afraid of?"

"Well, I have become so used to talking to you now, that I don't want to go back to the way it used to be, just me and the animals and birds. I enjoy being with you so much that I'm afraid I'd be lonely. I'm so scared that one day you won't need me anymore, and you won't see me or hear me call you. When I think about it, it makes me very sad." He hung his head and Nancy thought she saw a tear in his eye.

"Oh, you don't have to worry about that. I found you, and I'll always need you. You will always be my very own special friend."

"I hope so. But I still have this feeling."

Nancy looked down at where the snake had been lying on his back. The snake was gone. He had left so quickly and silently, no one had even heard him. She laughed, "Why, that old faker!"

* If you wish to read more about this different kind of snake, he is known as the Hog-nosed snake. He is also called Spreadhead or Puff Adder.

Chapter 5
SANDY GETS INTO MISCHIEF

A VERY SPECIAL FRIEND

Autumn was coming, the leaves were beginning to turn. Some of the trees looked as though they were on fire with their beautiful reds and yellows. The wind was becoming chilly at night, and Nancy worried about Sandy running around out there in the woods. She thought he was so clever the way he had made clothes out of anything he could find. He had woven together the hairs from the squirrels and rabbits to make a nice fur jacket. He used feathers, pine needles, grass, dried leaves. He had such an imagination. When it rained, a large leaf made a fine umbrella, and a discarded snake skin was perfect as a raincoat. But even with all the work Sandy went to making these things, they didn't last very long. They tore or fell apart, and he had to do it all over again. So that was why Nancy decided to try to make some clothes for her little friend. She had never tried anything like that before, so she wasn't sure how they would turn out.

It wasn't hard to get material. Her mother had given her some scraps. She thought Nancy was busy making doll clothes. She couldn't imagine what else could fit into clothes that tiny. She was glad to see Nancy busy and interested in something. It had been sad to see Nancy sitting around looking so unhappy. She had no way of knowing about the little tiny friend that had made such a difference in her daughter's life. Nancy hadn't told anyone about Sandy. She didn't want anyone to laugh at her. Sandy was just too special for that.

It made Nancy happy that Sandy seemed so proud of the new clothes. She could see him through the window as he strutted back and forth, admiring himself in the glass.

She had hardly turned away from the window when she heard a high-pitched scream, "Nancy, Nancy, help meeeeeee!!"

Running back to the window she caught sight of Rufus, the big yellow tomcat disappearing around the corner of the house.

Frightened, Nancy ran out the front door, just in time to see Sandy, screaming at the top of his lungs, go tearing by, just inches ahead of the big cat. She took off right behind them, yelling, "Rufus, Rufus, you stop that! Cut it out! You're going to hurt Sandy!" Rufus didn't pay any attention and didn't even slow down. The third time around the house Nancy finally caught up with them, grabbed Rufus by the fur on the back of his neck and yanked him off his feet. She shook him. "Rufus, just what do you think you're doing? Sandy isn't a mouse! Who ever heard of a red-headed mouse?"

Sandy collapsed against the wall, puffing and gasping for breath. Rufus still watched him closely and his tail jerked from side to side. "This isn't the first time he's tried to catch me. But the other times I always say him coming. This time I didn't. He came up behind me too fast. Look at the way he licks his lips. I think he's got the idea that I must taste good. But I really wouldn't. I think I'm much too tough! – Oh, look, Nancy! He tore my new pants with his claws. There's a big hole!"

Nancy put Rufus down and scolded him. "Rufus, I don't ever want to see you do that again. You leave Sandy alone, or I'll be very angry with you."

Rufus jerked his tail into the air and walked away. He lay down in the sun, but he kept watching Sandy through half-closed eyes. It was hard to tell if he was going to mind Nancy or not.

"Come on, Sandy. Climb up here on my lap. I still have my needle and thread. Let me fix your pants." Sandy climbed up and lay down across her knees, and she began to sew up the hole in the seat of his pants. "Don't worry, I'll be careful and not stick you with the needle. – You keep saying you can talk to the animals. Well, why don't you talk to Rufus and explain to him that you're not a mouse, and he can't have you for supper?"

Sandy let out a big sigh. "Talk to Rufus?

Sure, I'd like to do that. But the trouble is, Rufus won't stand still long enough. Every time he sees me – there he goes again. You can't talk to somebody if you're busy running for your life. I have more trouble with him that I ever had in the woods. I'm beginning to wonder if he'll listen to me anyway. All he seems to want to do is chase me. It's very depressing."

Nancy finished the sewing job. "I know what you mean. Cats are funny that way. It doesn't seem to matter what you want. They have a mind of their own and they just go ahead and do what they want anyway. If you can't get him to listen, you'll just have to stay out of his way. – Come on and get in my pocket and we'll go up to the garden. Daddy is plowing. Let's go watch. Maybe that will make you forget about the old cat."

With autumn coming, most of the garden was gone. Either eaten or canned or frozen for use during the winter. So now Nancy's father was plowing up part of it, so it would be ready to plant next year. They watched as he went up and down the rows. Some of the chickens that wouldn't stay in the pen were running around the garden, pecking and scratching the dirt, delighted with the bugs and worms that were being dug up.

Sandy climbed out of Nancy's pocket and jumped down. "I don't think there's anything that smells as good as fresh dirt." He ran out into the garden as Nancy warned him to be careful. He talked with the chickens, and ran and jumped over the rows, and fell down into the soft dirt. He would jump up laughing and start running again. He was having such a good time that he didn't see the tractor turning and starting toward him. Nancy screamed at him, but the tractor was making so much noise her voice was lost.

Sandy turned and fell down just as the tractor was coming closer. Nancy watched helpless as the tractor passed over him. The chickens ran in all directions, but he was not fast enough. One minute she saw his little red head and the next minute ... nothing! Her father just kept right on going. The tractor was too loud for him to hear anything.

Frightened, Nancy ran out into the soft dirt, stumbling and falling, making her way to where she last saw Sandy disappear. She called and called his name, and frantically started to dig.

Then just as suddenly as he had disappeared, she saw a little red head pop up from the dirt, with a little furry creature pushing him from behind. With a sigh of relief, she picked Sandy up and began brushing him off. She hurried out of the garden as the tractor started around again. "You really had me scared. I couldn't see you anywhere. You disappeared!"

He took a big deep breath. "You weren't the only one who was scared. I didn't know how I was going to get out of that. All I could see was those big wheels coming at me. But I fell down into a mole hole. That was him who pushed me out. He's pretty angry. He said all their tunnels down there are collapsing. He said he sure didn't have time to fool with me. – But just look at the new clothes you made for me. First I get them torn and now they're all dirty."

Nancy sat him down on top of a fence post by the pasture. "Don't worry about that, Sandy. I'll make you more if I have to. I'm just glad you're all right. Now, sit here and try to stay out of trouble."

Tony, the horse, saw Nancy and came running up to the fence. He put his head over the wire and gently nudged her. "Tony always wants me to pet him when I come out here. He likes to have his ears scratched. Have you ever noticed their noses are so soft? They feel like velvet. He always thinks I might have something for him to eat too. – You don't have to be afraid of him, Sandy."

"Oh, I'm not afraid of him. I would be able

to talk to him. He's not like that silly old Rufus, but I really prefer the smaller animals I'm used to in the woods. The horses and cows are so big it's hard for them to see me. I would just as soon stay out of their way." Sandy was still brushing the dirt out of his hair.

When Tony, the horse, saw that Nancy didn't have anything for him to eat, he decided to leave. As he turned to go, he bumped the fence post and Sandy fell over backwards. With a yell, he landed on the horse's back. Finding nothing to hold on to, he slid off and grabbed the tail. So Tony went walking off across the field, his tail swinging back and forth with Sandy hanging on for dear life, and screaming for Nancy.

"Oh, Sandy, not again!" Nancy yelled as she climbed through the wire and went running after the horse. Tony had not gone far before Sandy's hands began to slide down the tail. Finally, he couldn't hold on any longer and he fell to the ground. He lay there on his back as Nancy ran up to him. When she saw he wasn't hurt, she said, "Sandy, I don't know what's the matter with you. You just can't seem to stay out of trouble today."

Sandy sighed, "I know. It seems there are days like that. I think I'll just give up for today. – There's my friend, the woodpecker, up there. I'm going to see if he'll take me back to the hollow tree. I hurt all over. Maybe if I go back to bed things will be better tomorrow."

Sandy waved to the bird as it circled overhead. When it landed nearby, he crawled over and climbed up on its back. Laying his little head down wearily on its soft feathers, he waved good-bye to Nancy. She watched until the bird flew into the woods and disappeared from sight. Then she walked back toward the house. As she passed the garden, her father was still plowing as though nothing at all had happened.

Chapter 6
THE DUCKS AND THE TURTLE

Nancy was happily skipping along with a bucket in one hand and a fishing pole in the other, when she heard a little high-pitched voice calling her name. "Hey, Nancy, where are you going? Can I come along?"

She stopped and looked around, then she spotted the red hair among the leaves of a nearby tree. There was Sandy sitting on a low-hanging branch. "Oh, there you are, Sandy. Sure, you can come with me if you want to. I'm going to the pond. My brother, Tommy, has been trying to teach me how to catch fish. I'm not doing very well, so I'm going to practice. It's a lot harder than it looks."

Sandy climbed down and ran along beside her. "What are you going to catch fish for?"

"Why, they're good to eat. Of course, my Mom has to do the cooking part. Didn't you know that?"

"Well, I've not had much to do with fish. They are very hard to talk to down there in the water. But I do know that they are different from us, and they will die if you take them out of the water. I'm glad you're going to try to catch them for food thought, and not just for fun. The All-Over Spirit put a lot of creatures here to be used for food, but I think it's wrong to kill something just for fun. Animals deserve to live just as much as we do. Just because they're not as smart as we are shouldn't make any difference."

Nancy sat down in a shady spot by the pond and prepared her pole. "I've been digging worms all morning just the way Tommy showed me. That's the only part I don't like. But I'm getting pretty good at it. Now if I can just make the worm stop wiggling long enough to get him on the hook."

Sandy stood on a rock and looked out over the pond. There were several ducks swimming peacefully nearby. Frogs sat on the bank, and from time to time one would jump in with a noisy plop and sit on the water with just his eyes and the top of his head sticking out. The water rippled here and there as fish came up to the surface to catch an unsuspecting bug.

Sandy was standing with his hands on his hips when suddenly something caught his jacket and he was off his feet. And flying through the air. "Hey, what's going on! Nancy, help me! Helpppp!" he screamed. He flew high into the air and came down even faster and landed with a big splash right in the middle of the pond.

"Oh, Sandy, I'm sorry! I must have caught you with the fishhook. I guess I'm not very good at this yet. Sandy? Sandy? Where are you?" There were only ripples where he had disappeared under the water. Then with a big splash, a mop of red hair suddenly reappeared. Sandy screamed, his arms waving wildly in the air, he again disappeared beneath the surface. "Oh, Sandy, can't you swim?" Nancy was getting very worried. He was too far out for her to reach.

The head bobbed once again out of the water, and he began hitting the water wildly. "I never had to before!" That was all he managed to get out as he sunk again.

    The ducks had come in closer to see what was going on and were quacking loudly among themselves. This time as the exhausted little figure came up to the surface, the largest drake grabbed Sandy's clothes with his beak. He lifted the soaking wet little person out of the water and deposited him on the back of one of the ducks. She swam to the bank, and as she walked ashore, he rolled off her back and landed on the grass. All the ducks formed a circle around the quiet, wet figure, and began making an awful racket among themselves. Nancy pushed her way into the circle and removed the fishhook from his jacket. With tears in her eyes she picked up the limp body and began wiping the water from his face and hair.

"I'm sorry, Sandy, I didn't mean to do that. I guess I need a lot more practice. Are you all right?"

The little eyelids fluttered, and he breathed a big sigh. "Boy, I was really worried that time. I think I've had enough water to last me quite a while. I sure hope nothing like that ever happens again. But just to be on the safe side, maybe I'd better learn how to swim. I never had any reason to learn before."

He sat up and started wringing the water out of his hair and clothes. He looked up at all the ducks standing around him. "Boy, did you see what that big drake did? That was really quick thinking. I sure want to say thanks to all you fellas. If there's ever anything I can do to help you, I sure want to try. But I guess you don't have many problems living here in this nice pond. It looks so peaceful here."

All the ducks began to quack at once and started making a racket. "What are they saying, Sandy? They seem awfully excited about something," Nancy asked.

Sandy seemed surprised. "They say that I sure don't know what I'm talking about if I think they don't have any problems. I guess everybody has problems. They're just different kinds. They say it's not peaceful here, not at all. – I don't know what they're talking about, but they want to show me." He stood up and shook some more water out of his hair and squeezed out his pants. Then he followed the ducks over to the edge of the pond, with Nancy following close behind.

One of the ducks got in and swam over to a spot they had seemed to be avoiding before. As they watched she slowly moved in a circle. Suddenly she let out a loud squawk and was pulled down under the water by something no one could see. With much flapping of her wings she was able to free herself, and she swam quickly back to the others. Then they saw a dark head poke up from the water and glare at them. The ducks again began to quack wildly.

"So that's it, Nancy. There is a snapping turtle in there. He is very mean and dangerous. They are all afraid of him. He grabs the baby ducklings and pulls them under the water. And he snaps at the ducks' feet. A duck is very defenseless, and really has no way to protect itself except to fly away. But with this turtle it's hard to get away because they can't see him down there. They want to know if I can help them some way. I would sure like to, especially since their quick thinking may have saved my life. But I would want to help them anyway, because this kind of thing is so unfair."

Sandy stood in deep thought for several seconds, then walked to the edge of the pond. He called to the turtle, whose dark head was still out of the water. "Hey, you, you big bully! Come over here. I want to talk to you! Yes, you! That's all you are, a big bully!" The turtle glared at Sandy, and then slowly moved toward the bank. As he crawled out on the land the ducks backed quickly away. Sandy spoke to the creature, "Why are you doing these things to the ducks? You are acting like a bully. They are your neighbors. You can all live together in this pond. There is plenty of room and plenty of food for all of you. Why don't you try to get along together?" The turtle's only answer was to snap quickly at Sandy.

Sandy jumped so suddenly that he fell over backward. He sat there angrily watching as the turtle turned and crawled back into the water.

Nancy ran over and picked Sandy up. "What did he say to you?"

"Why, the nerve of him! He said to shut up and leave him alone, or he'd have me for dinner! Well, this is going to be a little harder than I thought." He went over to the ducks again. "I tell you, fellas, you're going to have to try something

The Ducks And The Turtle

different. He is picking on you because you won't fight back." They looked at each other puzzled and started quacking again. "I know, I know, you don't have any way to defend yourself. But that's what a bully usually does. He picks on someone weaker than himself. I guess it makes him feel big. One of you by yourself wouldn't be able to do anything, but what if you all organized? It would be awfully hard for him to fight all of you at the same time, wouldn't it? I know, it's always hard for creatures who are peaceful to think of doing something like that. But sometimes it's the only way. You don't like the way you have to live now, do you? Do you like to be afraid all the time? Well, then let's do something about it. Let's show that old bully. Now, I have a plan that might work. The ducks all crowded around Sandy as he whispered. Nancy couldn't hear what was going on. After a bit, he stopped, and they all walked over to the bank of the pond.

The turtle was now floating on top of the water. "Look at him. He's mighty sure of himself He's not even bothering to hide. He doesn't think we can do anything. Okay, let's do what I told you. You, the biggest drake, your job is to grab him and pull him up here on the bank. Turtles are slower and more helpless on land." The drake got into the water but hesitated and looked questioningly at Sandy. "I know, you're afraid he'll snap at you. But just do as I told you. Grab him by the tail. It's harder for him to turn his body and reach you that way."

The drake must have thought, "Oh, well, it <u>sounds</u> easy anyhow." The turtle floated lazily in the water and didn't even bother to look around at him. What did he have to worry about? He was the king of the pond. He could do anything he wanted. Everyone was afraid of him.

As the drake grabbed his tail, the turtle suddenly jumped. "How dare they? What did they think they were doing? Well, they had better not get him mad. He could be really mean when he got mad!" The turtle twisted and turned trying to snap at the drake, but he couldn't quite reach him. The drake held on stubbornly as he tugged and pulled him through the water and up onto the bank. He then let him loose. The turtle was very angry, and as the ducks and Sandy stood in a circle around him, he lashed out wildly and snapped in all directions. But this time nobody ran away. They just stood there surrounding him.

Sandy laughed, "He's saying we had better leave him alone or someone is going to get hurt. Now he's trying to get past us and get back into the water. Well, don't let him, fellas. Just keep him right here." Sandy tried to talk to the turtle and make him agree to live peacefully with the ducks. The turtle's only answer was to get madder and snap more furiously.

"Okay, he just won't listen to reason. Go ahead and do what I told you to." As Sandy watched, two of the drakes came up from behind the turtle, where they couldn't get bitten. They put their beaks under his shell and with a quick movement flipped the turtle over on his back. The ducks let out a cry of triumph. The turtle kicked and jumped but was unable to turn back over.

Sandy bent down and talked to him. "Well, how do you like feeling helpless? It's not much fun, is it? Do you know what will happen to you if we just leave you out here like this in the hot sun? You won't last very long. Turtles need the water."

The turtle began to look worried and he kicked harder than ever. He finally stopped, out of breath. "Yes, it will even be harder for you if you wear yourself out. What do you say? Do you want to try living in peace in the pond, or do you want to stay out here like this? It's up to you. I told you, there's plenty of food and plenty of room for everybody in this pond, and you ought to be able to get along together."

By this time the turtle was becoming scared. He didn't like the way the sun was heating up his shell. One of the greatest fears a turtle can have is to be turned over on his back. So, reluctantly, he finally agreed he would be willing to try.

When they heard this, the ducks flipped him back over onto his feet. He still looked very angry, but he was scared and wanted to get back into the safe water as quickly as possible. Sandy shouted after him as he crawled away, "Just remember, if you're thinking of getting even and hurting the ducks again, they know what to do now. They can grab you anytime you're not looking, and you'll end up on your back again. Next time they may not let you go again."

He spoke to the ducks, "I'll come back in a few days to see if everything is all right. But I think you have learned that you can work together, and he may not bother you anymore."

As Nancy and Sandy walked away the ducks seemed to be laughing. "I had better go home and get dried off," Sandy said. "And you know, Nancy, I don't think I want to go fishing with you anymore." He had a twinkle in his eye as he said that.

Chapter 7
THE ICY WINTER

Nancy was much happier now. The school had turned out to be a pretty nice place, as far as a school can be. There were many things to do. She liked the other kids and the teachers. But most of all, she had found a new friend, Diane. It was wonderful to find someone she could talk to again and share things with, just like Jeanne.

The winter had come and the snow and cold wind with it. She had not seen Sandy lately, and she was beginning to think maybe he was hibernating. Maybe he was sleeping through the cold weather like some animals do in the woods. During the night there had been an ice storm, so that meant there would be a short vacation from school. The school buses couldn't make it up the mountains when the heavy snows and ice came.

When Nancy woke up, she ran to the window and saw what looked like a wonderland. A layer of ice covered everything. It was the most beautiful thing she had ever seen. The limbs of the trees and even the tiniest blade of grass looked as though it were made out of glass. The rising sun shining on the ice made it sparkle with a thousand different colors, looking like a million diamonds and jewels scattered everywhere. She thought this was surely what Sandy meant about really looking at something and seeing the beauty and magic of it.

Then Nancy laughed. The chickens and ducks were trying to walk on the ice, and all they could do was slide. One duck decided it would be easier to fly, but when he tried to land, he just kept sliding. Even Rufus, the big yellow tomcat, was having problems. His feet kept going out from under him. It looked so funny. She started to go and eat breakfast when she saw a glimpse of red out of the corner of her eye. Turning around, she saw Sandy come sliding up to the window. He waved to her and she opened the window. As the cold air rushed in, she said, "What's the matter, Sandy? I thought you were sleeping like the animals. You look cold, the way you're shivering."

"No, I don't hibernate, but when it's cold I spend a lot of time trying to keep warm. But right now, I've got a problem. My hollow tree is warm enough, but now I can't get back up there. I slid and fell all the way down the tree this morning. When I tried to get back up, there was ice all over my steps. I don't know what I'm going to do. I went out to get some food. The squirrels and rabbits always share what they have with me. They always store plenty of food away for the winter."

Nancy thought, "Do you want me to carry you back there and put you in the tree?"

"No," he shook his head. "I don't think you will be able to walk on this ice any better that I can. All the animals are having trouble. Besides,

I'll have the same trouble again in the morning."

"Well, I guess you could stay here in my room for a few days."

"That would be a good idea. I never was in a house before. But it would only have to be until the ice melts, and I can climb the tree again." So, Nancy reached out the window and lifted Sandy into the house. He wandered around the room, his eyes wide with wonder, looking at everything. "I could see some of the room when I looked in the window, but I didn't know it was so big. Do you share it with the rest of the family?"

"No, this is my room. Tommy has his own room, and Mom and Daddy have theirs. This is just where I sleep. There is another room where we eat, and another one that's called a living room. That's where the fireplace is, and we can watch TV there."

"TV? What's that?" Sandy looked puzzled.

"Oh, you'll find out. You'll get to see a lot of new and strange things if you stay in a house for a while."

"I wonder why you people have to have so much room inside your house. My hollow tree is plenty big enough for me. But then, I have the whole woods to run around in. Maybe that's why you need so much room, because you don't spend as much time outside as I do."

"Well," Nancy said. "I have to go eat my breakfast or my Mom will get angry. You may come along if you want to but be careful, they don't see you. I don't know if they would understand about you."

"Well, I'm not worried. Most of the time people can't see me anyway. You were just different."

So, Sandy followed behind Nancy as she went to the kitchen. But he stayed close to the wall and in the shadows, just in case maybe someone might see him. He was worried that if something went wrong, he wouldn't have any place to stay, and it was awfully cold outside. Of course, there was always the rabbits' house back under the brush pile, or the moles' tunnels down underground. But most of the animals just went to sleep in the winter. That way they didn't have to worry about how cold it got in their home. Sandy had never been able to learn how to do that. Besides, it would be fun to stay in a house for a few days. He could learn a lot about people that way. Maybe it would help him to understand them better.

In the kitchen his curiosity finally got the better of him. There were so many things to see, he wanted to get a closer look at them. He climbed up on a chair, and after a few mishaps he finally made it up to the kitchen countertop. He ran along behind things as far as he could. Then he made a dash out into the open when he was sure no one was looking. From there he could see the pots boiling on the stove and could feel the heat. Very curious, he thought, "I wonder how they do that?"

It was hard for Nancy to eat her breakfast, as she watched Sandy out of the corner of her eye and hoped he wouldn't get into mischief. Now he was hiding behind the toaster, watching the water run out of the faucet into the sink. He thought that was fascinating. How could they get the water to come into the house?

Then suddenly the bread popped out of the toaster. He was so surprised and frightened, he jumped straight up into the air and when he came down, he slid off the counter to the floor. Sitting there dazed, he looked up to see Nancy's mother walking toward him with a plate of toast in her hand. Not knowing what to do, he dashed across in front of her to hide behind a broom on the other side of the room. She was startled. She screamed, and the plate and toast fell all over the floor.

Everyone turned to see what was the matter.

She was on her hands and knees picking up the mess and looking all around the room. "Didn't anybody else see that? I don't know what it was. I just saw a blur, but I think maybe a mouse has gotten into the house." Everyone laughed, because they hadn't seen anything. But Nancy was worried and tried to see where Sandy had gone to. Nancy's mother grabbed the broom to sweep up the broken pieces, and Sandy quickly disappeared around the corner of the refrigerator.

The rest of breakfast went quietly without any more interruptions. Nancy offered to clear off the table, because she wanted to be alone in the kitchen. She hadn't seen Sandy for a while and wondered where he was. She knew he had not left the kitchen, but where was he hiding? She carefully looked behind things and called his name softly so no one else would hear. She began to get worried. She couldn't find him anywhere. Where could he have gone so fast? The last time she had seen him, he was hiding by the side of the refrigerator. The refrigerator? Oh, no, could he? Mother had opened it to get some butter to make more toast. Oh, No! Nancy ran to it and jerked open the door. There sat the little red-haired figure crouched between the bottle of milk and the orange juice, shivering and shaking. She picked him up and held him in her hands to warm him.

"I thought I came into this house, so I could be warm," he said through chattering teeth. "You know, I'm beginning to think it's more dangerous in here than it is in the woods."

Nancy laughed. "You'll be all right if you just find a warm spot and try to stay out of mischief."

By the time Nancy was ready to go to bed that night Sandy was more than ready. He had spent a busy day exploring the house and watching the people. He had always wondered what people did in their houses all day. And then, there were those funny pictures that appeared in that box in the living room. That thing that Nancy called TV. It was very strange. It reminded Sandy a little bit of the All-Over Spirit, because his voice seemed to come out of nowhere like the voices in the box. But when the All-Over Spirit talked to him it was always something important or very wise. The voices in the box didn't seem very wise at all. In fact, some of the things he had seen and heard on the TV seemed very dumb. They didn't make much sense at all. But I guess it must have been important to the humans, they spent an awful lot of time watching it.

He had really liked the fireplace though. The fire was so nice and bright. It was the warmest he had felt since last summer. But he even had to be careful there. He fell asleep behind the woodpile and was rudely awakened when someone got some wood to throw in the fire. Yes, sir, a house was a dangerous place. He would sure have to be careful.

Sandy yawed and stretched. "Nancy, I've been looking around your room, and there's a lot of things I don't understand. Like, why do you have a little house inside of the big house." He pointed to the corner of the room.

"Oh, that's my old dollhouse. You can sleep in there tonight if you want to. There's a tiny little bed and covers and everything." They walked over to it and Nancy looked in the window. "I don't play with it anymore, but when I was little, I always wondered what it would be like to be little enough to live in there."

Sandy went inside and was looking around the rooms. "Oh, it's fine, all right. Everything is just my size. But I still think I like my hollow tree better. I am used to it. – I'm having a hard time understanding why you people have things like this that you can't possibly use. In fact, I guess that's probably what's bothering me the most. Why do you humans have so many <u>things</u>? You have things everywhere. I suppose some of them have a purpose, but a lot of them don't do anything but sit there. What's the reason for it?"

Nancy frowned, "You know, Sandy, now that you ask me, I'm not really sure I know the answer to that. A lot of the things we have really don't have a purpose. They are pretty, and they just sit there for us to look at. I guess we really don't need them. But didn't you say one time, when I asked you why you put dewdrops on the spider webs, that some things could exist just for the beauty and the pleasure it gives you to look at them?"

"That's right. I guess it's the same thing. Maybe it's because you don't live in the woods like I do. There is so much beauty around me out there, and it is changing all the time. All I need is a place to sleep and something to eat and a way to keep warm. There is always so much going on out there, I guess I never had to go looking for something pretty to look at. But you people, you close yourselves up in a house. You close out all the rest of the beautiful world. But I think you must miss it. Maybe that's why you try to bring bits and pieces of it inside. I don't know, it's a mystery. I think you people make things much more complicated than they have to be. It's supposed to be very simple. You humans are harder to understand than I thought you would be."

Suddenly there was a loud racket coming from another room in the house. Sandy put his hands over his ears and yelled over the noise, "What on earth is that?"

"That's just my brother, Tommy. He's got his stereo turned up too loud again. He's just playing music."

Sandy shook his head, held his ears and moaned, "Music? That's the last thing I would call it. Oh, my poor ears I think I'll take the music of the birds anytime, rather than that."

"Don't worry. I'll ask Tommy to turn it down." She said as she left the room.

Sandy moaned again. "You better, or I'll never get any sleep." He crawled into the little bed and pulled the tiny pillow over his head.

The next morning the sun came out bright and warm, and before long water was dripping from the house and pieces of ice were falling from the branches of the trees. Nancy got out of bed and went straight to the dollhouse, but Sandy wasn't there. She searched frantically around the room. He was so little, if he was sleeping somewhere else, he might get stepped on. Then suddenly, she saw the little red-haired figure run into the room, out of breath.

"Sandy, where have you been?"

He leaned against the wall and panted. "I'm going to leave and go back to my hollow tree as soon as I can."

Nancy was puzzled, "Why?" What's wrong?"

"Well, I was up early so I went in the other room to look around. I was climbing around on the shelves in there, when all of a sudden, I heard the awfullest noise you can imagine, and your mother came in with this big machine. I never heard anything like that in my life. It made my hair stand straight up. I was so scared!"

"Oh," Nancy laughed. "I'll bet that was the vacuum cleaner."

"Well, I don't know what it was, but I didn't think it was very funny. I got so scared that I knocked a book off the shelf. She saw it and started looking for me. When she pushed the books and things around on the shelf, I thought she was going to mash me for sure. But that's not the worst part." He stopped for breath. "I heard her tell your father that there must be a mouse in the house. She told him to let Rufus in! So, I better leave. I have enough trouble keeping away from him outside. I don't know if I could do it here. – Why does everyone think I'm a mouse?"

Nancy couldn't keep from laughing. "I'm sorry, Sandy, but it seems so funny. At least, it looks like the ice is melting outside, so you'll be able to get up into your hollow tree now. I guess if you have to go, you had better do it. But I sure hoped you would like living in a house."

"No, Nancy, things are just too different from what I'm used to. Things are too complicated, and everything is just too NOISY! I must get back to my tree and some peace and quiet. But at least I'll know where to come if I get too bored." Nancy helped him out of the window, and watched as he ran off toward the woods. She hoped he wouldn't get too cold out there by himself.

As Nancy turned from the window, she though, "Well, at least he got to have an adventure." Suddenly, Rufus came running into the room with a loud meow. "Well, Sandy, it looks like you got out of here just in time." She reached down and petted the big yellow tomcat as he smelled around the window. "Sorry, Rufus, you're too late. Sandy's gone back to where he belongs."

Chapter 8
THE PARTING

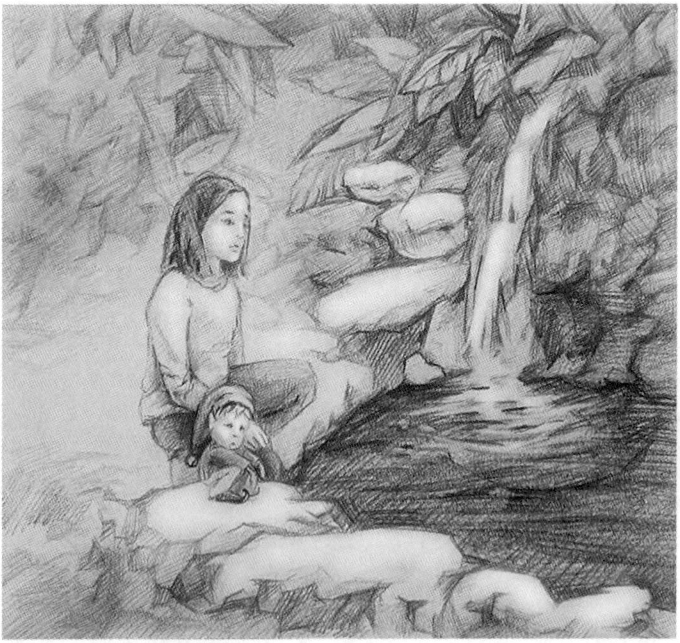

The Parting

Nancy ran through the woods toward her spring and breathed a sigh of relief as she caught a glimpse of red among the ferns. There was Sandy sitting on his rock with his chin cupped in his lands. She plopped down on the grass, out of breath. "Sandy, where have you been? I've been looking everywhere for you."

His voice seemed a little sad, "Oh, I've been around. I've been here."

She looked surprised. "You have? But I haven't seen you anywhere."

His eyes seemed much older than usual as he looked up at her and said softly 'I know. I know."

"But I don't understand," she seemed puzzled.

"Well, I knew this was coming, but I guess I just hoped it wouldn't. That maybe some way we could just go on the way we have been with no changes. But I should have known better. Life is full of changes." Nancy couldn't seem to understand what he was trying to say. "Lately you've been talking about your new friend, Diane, a lot, and about what you're doing at school. And I began to get worried. Then when you didn't see me when I pecked on your window, and you didn't hear me when I called you, I knew then that it was beginning. I got so sad and lonely. I didn't want to go back to the way it used to be, just me and the animals."

"Gee, Sandy, I'm sorry," Nancy muttered. "I didn't mean to do that. You know I would never hurt you for anything. I have been busy at school. I like it here so much more than I ever

A Very Special Friend

thought I would. I have made so many friends and I'm really happy again. I never thought I would ever find anyone to take Jeanne's place, but I was wrong. Diane is just as nice, and we can share everything the same way. But, Sandy, I love you too, and I don't understand how I could do that to you."

"That's all right. I always had the feeling that you would only be able to see me as long as you needed me. That one day you would outgrow me. So, you see, it's perfectly natural. You're beginning to grow up."

Nancy began to cry. "But, Sandy, if that's what it means to grow up, that I will lose you … then I don't ever want to grow up."

"Well, I'm afraid that's something you won't be able to stop. You might as well try to hold back the night or keep the sun from rising in the morning. It's something that has to happen. Nothing ever stays the same. But don't be sad. It won't happen tonight or tomorrow. It won't happen suddenly, that would be cruel. It will happen slowly and gradually, the way it is beginning to now. You will just not need me as often, so you will see me less and less. And then one day I will not be around anymore. But by that time, it won't matter, because your life will be full of so many wonderful things. And I will be just a happy memory of your lonely time. The time when you needed someone."

She wiped he eyes. "Well, maybe it will be easier that way. But you have taught me so many wonderful things. What if I don't remember them if you're not here to remind me?"

"No knowledge is ever lost. That is why you must learn as much as you can. When you learn something, it will stay with you. You may not be aware of it, but it is there and will come back when you need it. Be sure to remember one lesson above all others that I taught you. Really look at things. See the world, hear it, feel it, smell it, and enjoy the beauty all around you."

"But, Sandy, what about you? You said you would be lonely. That you didn't want to go back to the way it was before, just you and the animals. What will happen to you?" She couldn't bear the thought of her little friend being unhappy.

"Well, that was what I was afraid of at first. But then the All-Over Spirit came and talked with me. He said he likes the way I have learned to live with humans. It would be a shame to lose that. Once you have learned something, it is very difficult to return to the way you were before. So, I guess you would say that He gave me a promotion. I will be allowed to continue to help people as well as my other duties. I thought I had nothing left to learn, but I found out that is not true. I have learned a great lesson from you."

Nancy looked surprise. "From me? How could you ever learn anything from me?"

"Well, do you remember when I told you that the greatest magic of all was the magic of life?" She nodded. "Well, I was wrong"

"How could you ever be wrong about anything?"

He cocked his little head. "Well, it just shows that you never know it all. You can always learn something new and exciting, if you just open up your heart. Being with you I have learned the lesson of <u>love</u>. And I have discovered that love is the greatest magic of all. Because what is life without love? To be alive is a great and wonderful thing, but I have found it is empty without love. It is the greatest gift of all, and it is free to everyone. But we must each one find it ourselves. No one can do it for us. The All-Over Spirit has shown me that to try to hold on to you when you no longer need me is a selfish kind of love. To really love someone, you must be able to let them go when the time comes, no matter how much it hurts."

Nancy smiled, "You mean that I was really able to teach you all that? I loved you, but I thought it was a natural thing. The same way that I love my folks."

"And He told me that love is very funny. Real love just kind of bubbles up inside of you and spills out. It has to be shared with others. So, this is what He wants me to do, to spread it around. He told me to get on my woodpecker and fly over to the next farm. Have you met the people who moved in there?"

"No, not yet. I heard there were some new neighbors and that they have a little boy. But I also heard he doesn't go to school, so I haven't met him yet. Why?"

"Well, I went over there and peeked in the window. There is a little boy there, and he sits in a funny-looking chair with wheels. That's the reason he can't go to school. He doesn't have any brothers or sisters. He looked so sad and lonely. And you know what? I have this feeling that maybe ... maybe he will be able to see me."

Nancy smiled, "Oh, Sandy, that would be wonderful. If he could see you like I can, then he wouldn't be lonely any more either. I wouldn't mind sharing you with someone else. But it makes me sad to think that someday I won't be able to see you anymore. I don't want to forget you."

Sandy patter her hand, "Well when the time comes, just remember me sometimes. Because when you remember me, for that little brief moment, I will live again in your memory. We will always be alive if we are remembered. –

When you see the dewdrops on the spider webs, and the leaves bursting into color in the fall, then think of me. When you see the moonbeams peeking through the clouds, and a dozen little fireflies dancing on the lawn, then think of me. Think of me, and I will never die!"

The End

About The Author

Dolores Cannon, a regressive hypnotherapist and psychic researcher who recorded "Lost" knowledge, was born in 1931 in St. Louis, Missouri. She was educated and lived in St. Louis until her marriage in 1951 to a career Navy man. She spent the next 20 years traveling all over the world as a typical Navy wife and raising her family. In 1970 her husband was discharged as a disabled veteran, and they retired to the hills of Arkansas. She then started her writing career and began selling her articles to various magazines and newspapers. She has been involved with hypnosis since 1968, and exclusively with past-life therapy and regression work since 1979. She has studied the various hypnosis methods and thus developed her own unique technique which enabled her to gain the most efficient release of information from her clients. Dolores taught her unique technique of hypnosis all over the world.

In 1986 she expanded her investigations into the UFO field. She has done on-site studies of suspected UFO landings and has investigated the Crop Circles in England. The majority of her work in this field has been the accumulation of evidence from suspected abductees through hypnosis.

Dolores was an international speaker who had lectured on all the continents of the world. Her nineteen books are translated into twenty languages. She has spoken to radio and television audiences worldwide. And articles about/by Dolores have appeared in several U.S. and international magazines and newspapers. Dolores was the first American and the first foreigner to receive the "Orpheus Award" in Bulgaria, for the highest advancement in the research of psychic phenomenon. She has received Outstanding Contribution and Lifetime Achievement awards from several hypnosis organizations.

Dolores had a very large family who kept her solidly balanced between the "real" world of her family and the "unseen" world of her work.

If you wish to correspond with Ozark Mountain Publishing, Inc. about Dolores' work or her training classes, please submit to the following address. (Please enclose a self-addressed stamped envelope for their reply.) Dolores Cannon, P.O. Box 754, Huntsville, AR, 72740, USA or email the office at decannon@msn.com or through our website:www.ozarkmt.com

Dolores Cannon, who transitioned from this world on October 18, 2014, left behind incredible accomplishments in the fields of alternative healing, hypnosis, metaphysics, and past life regression, but most impressive of all was her innate understanding that the most important thing she could do was to share information. To reveal hidden or undiscovered knowledge vital to the enlightenment of humanity and our lessons here on Earth. Sharing information and knowledge is what mattered most to Dolores. That is why her books, lectures and unique QHHT® method of hypnosis continue to amaze, guide and inform so many people around the world. Dolores explored all these possibilities and more while taking us along for the ride of our lives. She wanted fellow travelers to share her journeys into the unknown.

Other Books by Ozark Mountain Publishing, Inc.

Dolores Cannon
A Soul Remembers Hiroshima
Between Death and Life
Conversations with Nostradamus, Volume I, II, III
The Convoluted Universe -Book One, Two, Three, Four, Five
The Custodians
Five Lives Remembered
Jesus and the Essenes
Keepers of the Garden
Legacy from the Stars
The Legend of Starcrash
The Search for Hidden Sacred Knowledge
They Walked with Jesus
The Three Waves of Volunteers and the New Earth
A Vey Special Friend
Aron Abrahamsen
Holiday in Heaven
James Ream Adams
Little Steps
Justine Alessi & M. E. McMillan
Rebirth of the Oracle
Kathryn Andries
Cat Baldwin
Divine Gifts of Healing
The Forgiveness Workshop
Penny Barron
The Oracle of UR
Dan Bird
Finding Your Way in the Spiritual Age
Waking Up in the Spiritual Age
Julia Cannon
Soul Speak – The Language of Your Body
Ronald Chapman
Seeing True

Jack Churchward
Lifting the Veil on the Lost Continent of Mu
The Stone Tablets of Mu
Patrick De Haan
The Alien Handbook
Paulinne Delcour-Min
Spiritual Gold
Holly Ice
Divine Fire
Joanne DiMaggio
Edgar Cayce and the Unfulfilled Destiny of Thomas Jefferson Reborn
Anthony DeNino
The Power of Giving and Gratitude
Carolyn Greer Daly
Opening to Fullness of Spirit
Anita Holmes
Twidders
Aaron Hoopes
Reconnecting to the Earth
Patricia Irvine
In Light and In Shade
Kevin Killen
Ghosts and Me
Donna Lynn
From Fear to Love
Curt Melliger
Heaven Here on Earth
Where the Weeds Grow
Henry Michaelson
And Jesus Said – A Conversation
Andy Myers
Not Your Average Angel Book
Guy Needler
Avoiding Karma
Beyond the Source – Book 1, Book 2
The History of God

For more information about any of the above titles, soon to be released titles, or other items in our catalog, write, phone or visit our website:
PO Box 754, Huntsville, AR 72740|479-738-2348/800-935-0045|www.ozarkmt.com

Other Books by Ozark Mountain Publishing, Inc.

The Origin Speaks
The Anne Dialogues
The Curators
Psycho Spiritual Healing
James Nussbaumer
And Then I Knew My Abundance
The Master of Everything
Mastering Your Own Spiritual Freedom
Living Your Dram, Not Someone Else's
Gabrielle Orr
Akashic Records: One True Love
Let Miracles Happen
Nikki Pattillo
Children of the Stars
Victoria Pendragon
Sleep Magic
The Sleeping Phoenix
Being In A Body
Charmian Redwood
A New Earth Rising
Coming Home to Lemuria
Richard Rowe
Imagining the Unimaginable
Exploring the Divine Library
Garnet Schulhauser
Dancing on a Stamp
Dancing Forever with Spirit
Dance of Heavenly Bliss
Dance of Eternal Rapture
Dancing with Angels in Heaven
Manuella Stoerzer
Headless Chicken
Annie Stillwater Gray
Education of a Guardian Angel
The Dawn Book
Work of a Guardian Angel

Joys of a Guardian Angel
Blair Styra
Don't Change the Channel
Who Catharted
Natalie Sudman
Application of Impossible Things
L.R. Sumpter
Judy's Story
The Old is New
We Are the Creators
Artur Tradevosyan
Croton
Jim Thomas
Tales from the Trance
Jolene and Jason Tierney
A Quest of Transcendence
Paul Travers
Dancing with the Mountains
Nicholas Vesey
Living the Life-Force
Dennis Wheatley/ Maria Wheatley
The Essential Dowsing Guide
Maria Wheatley
Druidic Soul Star Astrology
Sherry Wilde
The Forgotten Promise
Lyn Willmott
A Small Book of Comfort
Beyond all Boundaries Book 1
Beyond all Boundaries Book 2
Stuart Wilson & Joanna Prentis
Atlantis and the New Consciousness
Beyond Limitations
The Essenes -Children of the Light
The Magdalene Version
Power of the Magdalene

For more information about any of the above titles, soon to be released titles, or other items in our catalog, write, phone or visit our website:
PO Box 754, Huntsville, AR 72740|479-738-2348/800-935-0045|www.ozarkmt.com